OVER THE SEAS AND FAR AWAY;
SAIL IN A BOAT FOR ALL OF A DAY

To Mark and Heather who got the drift & Tammie and Patrick who got the message

First published 1996

3 5 7 9 10 8 6 4 2

© Mairi Hedderwick 1996

Mairi Hedderwick has asserted
her right under the Copyright, Designs and Patents Act, 1988
to be identified as the author and illustrator of this work

First published in the United Kingdom 1996
by The Bodley Head Children's Books
Random House, 20 Vauxhall Bridge Road, London SW1V 2SA

Random House UK Limited Reg. No. 954009

A CIP catalogue record for this book
is available from the British Library

ISBN 0 370 32442 0

Printed in China

THE BIG
KATIE MORAG
STORYBOOK

Mairi Hedderwick

The Bodley Head

Gertrude Isobel Tibsley (Bel)
(Historian & Crofter)   M.   Capt. Nils J. Olsen
(Helicopter pilot)

GRANNIE
ISLAND

Sven & Sean Olsen (TWINS)
(Singer & Cellist)

Isobel Olsen   M.   Peter McColl
(Post mistress)   (Shopkeeper)

Katie Morag McColl   Liam McColl   Flora Ann McColl

KATIE MORAG

Katie Morag's Family Tree

Grace Margaret Nicol (Meg)
(Retired Nurse & Secretary)

GRANMA MAINLAND

M. Hector Archibald McColl (1)
(Butcher - deceased)

Neilly Beag (2)
(Crofter)

James McColl M. Rachel Stoddart
(Reverend)

Matthew McColl
(Whereabouts unknown)

Hector McColl   Archie McColl   Dougal McColl   Jamie McColl   Murdo Iain McColl

THE BIG BOY COUSINS

Lady of the Isles.

KATIE MORAG'S ISLAND

Katie Morag's island is called the Isle of Struay. Nobody can walk to Katie Morag's island, or take a bus or a train. The only way to go is by boat.

The *Lady of the Isles* comes three times a week bringing all the things the islanders need: letters and parcels, newspapers and magazines, provisions for the shop, supplies for the Struachs. Visitors come that way too.

If it is very stormy no boat comes at all.

"An island is a piece of land with water all around," says the captain of the *Lady of the Isles.*

"An island is also the top of a mountain sticking out of the sea," says Grannie Island, who is very wise.

All the islanders have little boats. Little boats must hug the land; big boats can sail far away to distant places. The mainland is very distant. That is where Granma Mainland lives – some of the time.

Granma Mainland is a High-flyer.

Neilly Beag smiles up at the sky. "You *can* go another way to a wee island," he reminds everyone.

"But boats are best," mutters Grannie Island.

Katie Morag smiles. She loves both of her grandmothers just the same.

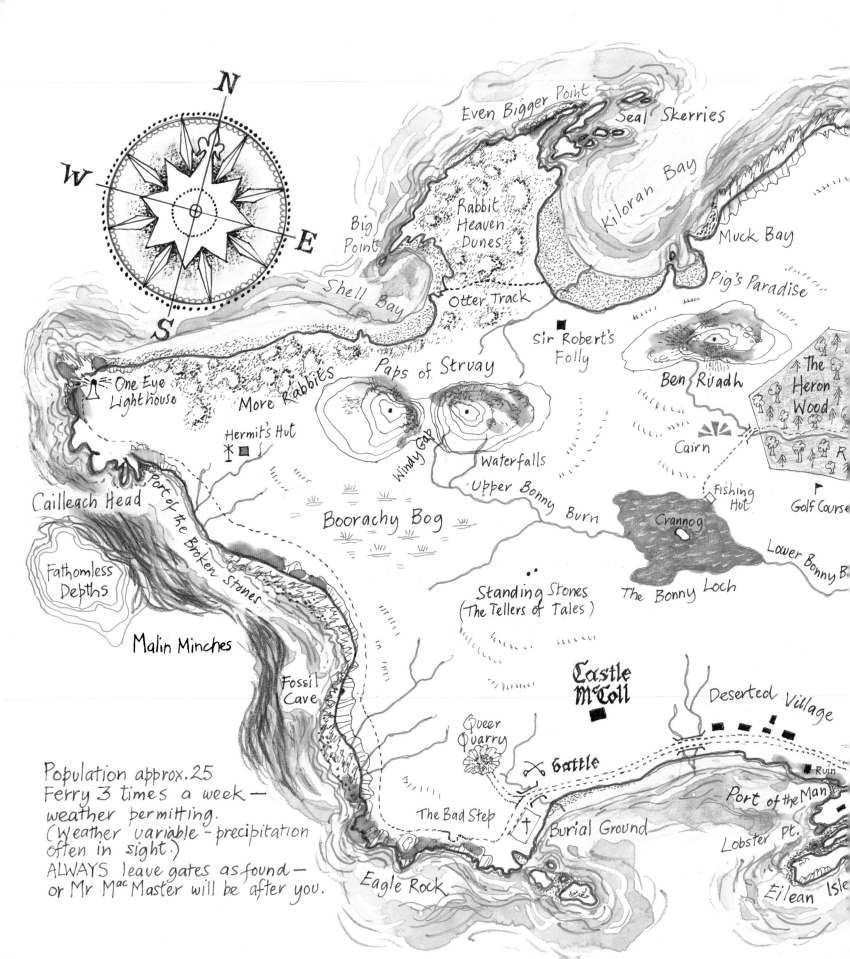

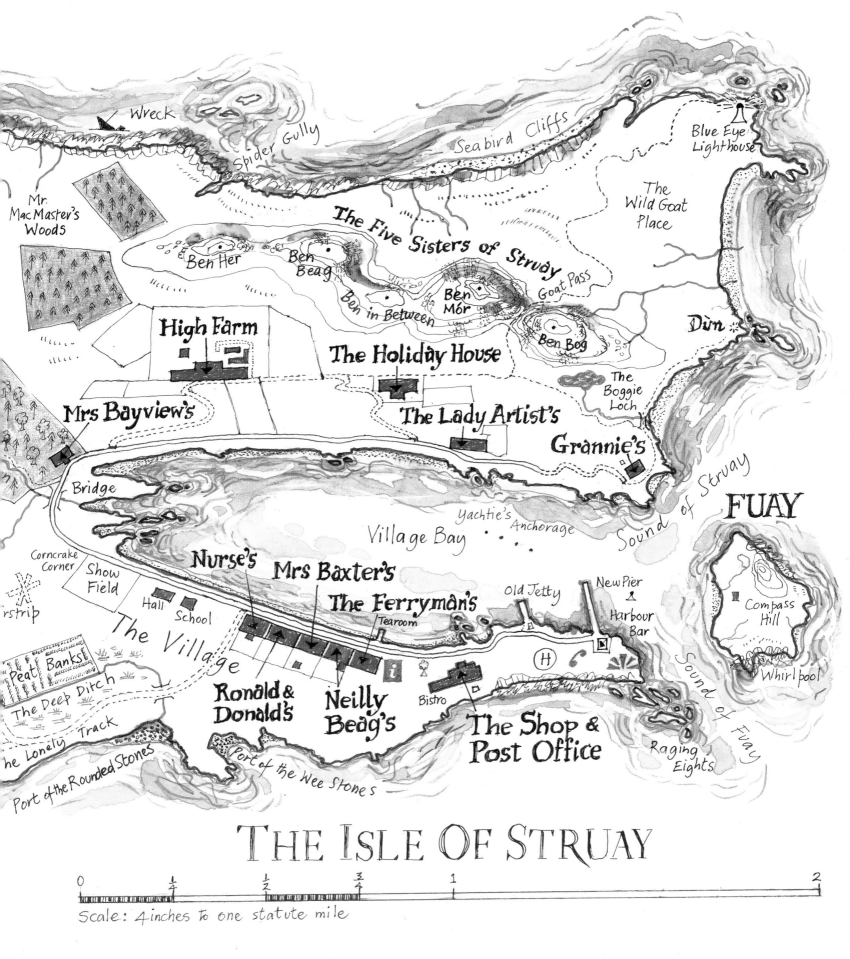

Wreck

Spider Gully

Seabird Cliffs

Blue Eye Lighthouse

The Wild Goat Place

Mr. MacMaster's Woods

The Five Sisters of Struay

Ben Her

Ben Beag

Ben in Between

Ben Mór

Goat Pass

Ben Bog

Dùn

High Farm

The Holiday House

The Boggie Loch

Mrs Bayview's

The Lady Artist's

Grannie's

Bridge

Sound of Struay

FUAY

Yachtie's Anchorage

Village Bay

Corncrake Corner

Show Field

Nurse's

Mrs Baxter's

The Ferryman's

Old Jetty

New Pier

Harbour Bar

Compass Hill

Hall

School

Tearoom

Bistro

(H)

Sound of Fuay

rstrip

The Village

Peat Banks

The Deep Ditch

Ronald & Donald's

Neilly Beag's

The Shop & Post Office

Raging Eights

Whirlpool

he Lonely Track

Port of the Rounded Stones

Port of the Wee Stones

THE ISLE OF STRUAY

0   ¼   ½   ¾   1   2

Scale: 4 inches to one statute mile

WINDY WEATHER

The West winds blow to Struay Isle;
Smirring rain and clouds the while.

EAST   WEST

The South winds blow and warm the sea;
'Fine to paddle,' say Liam and me.

The East winds blow and nip our ears;
Liam's freezing, close to tears.

HOME's BEST

The North winds blow and we feel snow.
Time for home; it's off we go.

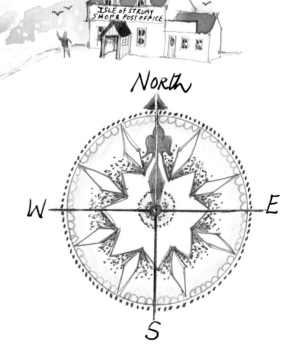

THE BAKING DAY SECRET

Friday is baking day on the Isle of Struay.

That is the day Katie Morag likes to go visiting in the Village. I wonder why?

"Take Liam," said Mrs McColl one particular Friday.

But Katie Morag thought that was a very bad idea.

"I'll keep the bowls for you to lick," her mother promised. Mrs McColl was not a good baker. Licking the bowls was often the best bit of her baking.

Annoyed, Katie Morag pushed Liam towards the first house in the Village. "He'll know my secret now and ALWAYS want to come," she frowned.

The ferryman's wife made quite the most fabbydoo chocolate cakes. "Come to try my new recipe, Katie Morag?" she smiled, as Liam and Katie Morag appeared at the door.

"Oh no!" fibbed Katie Morag. "We've just come to say 'hello'.

Say 'hello' Liam..."

"That's strange," thought the ferryman's wife to herself. Katie Morag always sat down and enjoyed her Friday visits. "Here's a couple of pieces, then, to take home, since you won't have them now," she said in surprise as she put two large slices of cake into a bag. Liam licked his lips.

"Thank you very much," said Katie Morag.

"Want eat!" said Liam, hopefully, when they got outside.

"Certainly NOT!" Katie Morag was firm. Liam must not find out about the Baking Day secret.

Neilly Beag and Granma Mainland were in the next house. What meringues Neilly could bake! Mounds of shiny white spirals sat drying by the stove. The cream for in-between was whipped up stiff.

"Test the best yet, Katie Morag!" he beamed.

"Oh no!" said Katie Morag. "We've just come to say 'hello'!" Katie Morag's mouth was watering.

"That's very odd..." thought Neilly. "Well, you can take some for later, can't you?" he suggested, fetching out a bag.

Maybe it was not so bad Liam coming along, thought Katie Morag. She had never been given *bags* of baking before.

By the time Katie Morag reached the last house in the village, Liam had had to give up his seat in the bogie. Nurse had just finished making syrupy sweet porridgies.

"Perfect timing – have a bite!" Nurse offered the tray.

Of course when Katie Morag refused as usual, Nurse filled yet another bag. Liam was waiting eagerly to take it.

"Want eat NOW!" demanded Liam as they headed homewards, the bogie laden with cake and meringues, doughnuts, shortbread and porridgies.

"NO!" said Katie Morag angrily. She was wondering where she could hide all the bags without Liam seeing.

When the two of them got back home, Katie Morag hid the bogie round the corner of the house. The kitchen of the Shop and Post Office was in a terrible mess. Pots and jugs, spoons and bowls were all over the place.

Burnt biscuits and buns, soggy sunk sponges and leather-hard pancakes were scattered on the table. Mrs McColl was in tears by the sink. The baby was covered in flour.

"The new teacher and his wife are coming to tea," wailed Mrs McColl in despair. "What am I going to give them to eat?"

Katie Morag and Liam looked at each other, reluctantly.

Suddenly, "We've got lots of baking for a scrumptious tea," said Katie Morag.

"How *kind* of the Villagers," sniffed Mrs McColl. "Maybe they'll teach me how to bake one day?"

It did not take long to tidy everything up. The tea party with the new teacher and his wife was a great success. Katie Morag and Liam were very polite and only ate what they were offered. They were so happy to see Mrs McColl happy again.

"What wonderful bakers you islanders are!" praised the new teacher.

"Well, I have a lot to learn," replied Mrs McColl, graciously. She was being very honest, don't you think?

"You are my very best friends!" said Mrs McColl after the visitors had gone. "I think you deserve a special treat! Off to bed, the two of you!"

Katie Morag and Liam looked bewildered – that was no treat...

But it was. One bag of baking had been missed in the rush to tidy the kitchen. It was Nurse's super, syrupy-sweet porridgies. Mrs McColl said they could have them for a midnight feast if they promised to brush their teeth after. They promised.

Katie Morag and Liam never went to bed quicker than on the night of the Baking Day Secret.

Once all the house was quiet and the stars peeping in the window they began their feast by torchlight. They even left some over for the next day. They had to... they were so full.

RECIPE FOR PORRIDGIES

Pre-heat oven to Gas Mark 3 or 300°F or 110°C (or when the needle reaches 8 o'clock on Grannie Island's stove).

Grease a 20cm x 30cm (8" x 12") shallow baking tray.

Ingredients:

100g (4oz) butter
75g (3oz) soft brown sugar
30ml (2 tablespoons) syrup
200g (8oz) rolled oats
pinch of salt

Melt butter in a large pan over a low heat.
Add sugar and syrup and salt. Mix well.
Stir in rolled oats. Mix very well.

Spread mixture evenly in tray with palette knife.
Bake for 25-35 minutes, till goldie brown.
Take out of oven. Let cool a little.
Mark in squares or fingers with knife.
Leave in tray till cold. Put
pieces in an airtight tin.

Katie Morag likes them
best when still warm.

TIRESOME TED SEA SHANTIES

KATIE MORAG HAS LOST HER TED

Katie Morag has lost her Ted
And can't tell where to find him.
Leave him alone and he'll come home,
The wind and the tide behind him.

Of All The Fish That Swim In The Sea

Of all the fish that swim in the sea,
The Tiresome Ted is the one for me.

A Herring's no use to cuddle in bed;
Cuddle a herring? I'd rather be dead!

Mackerels are slippery, most used for bait,
Some doused in vinegar, six to a plate.

Flounders are flatfish; that everyone knows,
But under the sand they nibble your toes.

Eels have got teeth, sharp set in their jaw.
Down deep a-snaking – is that what I saw?

The Cod is the King and that's no mistake,
But sooner or later he's just plain fishcake.

Of all the fish that swim in the sea,
The Tiresome Ted is the one for me.

WHAT SHALL SHE DO?

What shall she do
With a soaking teddy
Washed up on the seashore?

Hang him on the washline
Till he's fluffy;
Wind and sun together.

Put him by the fireside
Till he's cosy;
In your Grannie's kitchen.

Feed him mince and tatties
Till he's pudgy;
Put him on his potty.

Brush his fur and comb him
Till he's lovely;
In the baby's nightie.

Sing a lullaby song
Till he's sleepy.
Then take him into bed.

GRANNIE ISLAND IS ILL

When Grannie Island took ill Mr and Mrs McColl became very worried. "She can't stay over there all alone," exclaimed her daughter, Mrs McColl. "She'll have to come to us until she gets better."

Mr McColl groaned.

Katie Morag was very sorry that her Grannie was not well but thought it would be great fun having her to stay. "We will read her stories," she told Liam, "and we will sit on her bed."

Immediately Grannie Island heard of these plans she was adamant. "East, West – home's best!" she stated firmly. "Go away! I'll be fine – stop fussing."

This meant that the McColls had to go over to Grannie Island's house on the other side of the bay every day to feed, not only Grannie Island but her dog, the cats, the sheep, the hens, ducks and geese. The animals and birds missed Grannie Island and were awkward.

"You are being awkward too!" scolded Mrs McColl. "How can we get on with running the Shop and Post Office if you behave like this?"

Katie Morag said she would stay and look after Grannie Island. "You are far too young!" snapped Mrs McColl. And that was the end of that.

Then Mrs McColl had an idea. Granma Mainland and Neilly Beag had just come back to the island. "The very person to take care of Grannie Island!" thought the McColls. Granma Mainland had been a nurse in her younger days.

"*Now* can I go to Grannie Island's and help?" pleaded Katie Morag. Katie Morag knew that the two grandmothers did not always get on too well.

"As long as you don't get in the way," said her mother.

Whilst Neilly was spring-cleaning the Village house Granma Mainland was intent on doing the same at Grannie Island's.

"Dreadful mess!" she muttered. "And where is the Hoover and the washing machine?"

Grannie Island did not have such things. Helplessly she watched as Granma Mainland took over her home, fussing and cleaning. The dustbin was soon very full.

But as the days passed Grannie Island began to perk up. It was funny to see Granma Mainland on her hands and knees scrubbing the kitchen floor. She had to take off all her fancy clothes and jewellery. Grannie Island's old slippers did not quite suit her.

And when it came to feeding the animals and birds, that was the funniest thing of all – Granma Mainland in Wellingtons and overalls! Grannie Island peeked out of the bedroom window and laughed until her sides were sore.

This made Granma Mainland very angry and she would come in and plump up Grannie Island's pillows abruptly and give her only *one* biscuit with her cup of tea.

When Granma Mainland was not looking, Katie Morag raided the tin and hid extra biscuits under the mattress.

"Where do all these crumbs come from?" fretted Granma Mainland as she swept under the bed for the umpteenth time.

Katie Morag did all the best things for Grannie Island: reading her stories, drawing pictures, turning the tapes on the cassette, helping with the jigsaw and, best of all, helping to eat up the biscuit and grape supplies.

For the most part, everyone got on well and Grannie Island was definitely improving. Evenings were best when Granma Mainland sat down at last. That was when she put her earrings and her high-heeled shoes back on and chatted lovingly to Neilly Beag on the phone.

Katie Morag would be snug on Grannie Island's
bed reading her favourite book and the dog and
the cats were finally allowed into the house –
if their paws were clean.

KATIE MORAG
DELIVERS THE MAIL

It was a time of rainbows on the island. The McColls came over one shimmery Sunday to see how everyone was getting on. Grannie Island was back on her feet. The animals and birds were happy again. Granma Mainland was resting on the couch, filing her hard-worked nails and massaging her ankles. Grannie Island's house was spotless.

"There is gold at the end of the rainbow," Katie Morag told Liam as they played outside. "I wish we could find it, don't you?" But no matter how fast they ran they could not catch the rainbow's end. It always moved on – up over the Lady Artist's chimney pot, past the McMasters' stable, through Mrs Bayview's greenhouse, into the deepest part of the Bonny Loch and then far out to sea.

Mrs McColl called them in for tea.

"Grannie Island says she is quite better now. You and Liam can stay with her tonight. We'll take Granma Mainland back to the Village."

Grannie Island thanked Granma Mainland for all her help. She was being polite. Grannie Island actually hated Granma Mainland's fancy cooking, and even more, all her tidying.

What a good mood Grannie Island was in after the McColls and Granma Mainland left. "Now let's get everything back in its place," she smiled.

The dog and the cats were let in immediately and leapt to their favourite cushions. Katie Morag and Liam loved setting out all the odds and ends that Granma Mainland had swept away into boxes and bags.

At supper time they all feasted on mince and tatties and mashed tumshie. "Can't stand that tagliatelle stuff of Granma Mainland's – slides all over the plate," said Grannie Island.

Next morning, Katie Morag and Liam packed their rucksacks. It was time to go. Much as Katie Morag had enjoyed being at Grannie Island's, she looked forward to going home.

"Where are my old photos?" Grannie Island was still searching. "My favourite one is missing!" she wailed.

"Here comes Granma Mainland!" called Katie Morag from the open door, relieved. "She'll know..."

"I don't want that woman in my house ever again!" shouted Grannie Island. "Bossing and losing my things..."

But Granma Mainland was not in a bossy mood. She was very, very upset. "I've lost my favourite and most expensive gold earrings. They must be here!"

She stood, aghast, at the returned chaos of Grannie Island's house. "I'll never find them in all this mess! How could you?"

Katie Morag and Liam thought it best to get out of the house until the two grandmothers had calmed down and, hopefully, found their precious possessions.

Another rainbow appeared in the sky. It was very close; so close, in fact, that the end of it was definitely in Grannie Island's dustbin. This time Katie Morag and Liam moved like lightning head-first into the bin before the rainbow disappeared.

Gold *did* glitter in amongst the rubbish... Granma Mainland's earrings! And underneath the rest of the junk, the box of old photos! There was also a brightly knitted tea cosy that Liam fancied for a hat and a tiny little wooden horse that Katie Morag knew would love to sit on her window-sill.

Cries of delight met Katie Morag and Liam as they raced, rather grubbily, into the house with the rainbow treasures.

The two grandmothers apologised to each other and, of course, Grannie Island said Katie Morag and Liam could keep the hat and the horse.

OLD PHOTOS

Once Grannie Island had put her favourite photo back on the jam-packed sideboard she walked everyone along the road a bit before saying "Goodbye" and "Thank you".

Granma Mainland's earrings glinted in the sun as she turned to wave. Katie Morag and Liam waved too and then everyone headed homeward, their precious possessions safe and sound.

But Katie Morag's most special possession was knowing that she and Liam had caught the rainbow's end.

THE CATS OF STRUAY

Scratch Patch is the mother of them all.
She *loves* having kittens just because...

Haggis Virginia *sleeps* on the hamster cage
– just in case...

Justeenie loves Big Cat – just teenie, of course...

Jake is the thief – isn't that JUST awful?

Mr Mistake is – just a mistake...

Freddie is *FEROCIOUS* – just as well...

FaBbyDoo is a mouser – just in time?

Pussy Willow is a knitter – just for fun...

Charlie is the purrer – just to please...

And Seamus is the father of them all – just because...

SUMMER VISITORS

Many visitors come on holiday to the island in the summer. Katie Morag's mother and father are forever emptying boxes and stacking shelves, polishing the counter and fussing around the Holiday People. Katie Morag gets very bored.

One summer, Mrs McColl decided to make a fancy arrangement in the shop window for the visitors to admire.

"Go down to the shore, Katie Morag, for some sand and seaweed. Just to add the finishing touch," said Mrs McColl as she stacked a pyramid of beach-balls under an archway of buckets and spades. "And anything else that would look good," she added.

Katie Morag shovelled a layer of sand and then a layer of seaweed into her bogie. She scanned the tide line. Further along the shore there was something strange. Dark and shiny, it looked like a wet rumpled jacket; but it was moving. The sleeve bit was waving at her. Katie Morag was more interested than frightened. What could have been buttons seemed more like eyes and, sure enough, when Katie Morag got closer the buttons blinked.

"A baby seal!" cried Katie Morag. She looked out to sea. The mother must be hunting for fish in the bay. Katie Morag looked long and hard. But no head bobbed up out of the waves to check all was well with the pup.

The seal pup stared at Katie Morag with large appealing eyes.

"You would look very good in the seaside display!" thought Katie Morag. Suddenly the shop was an exciting place to be, "I'll look after you," said Katie Morag. "I'll call you Ròn."

"Take that seal back where he belongs!" exclaimed Mrs McColl. "He is most definitely NOT going in my window display!"

Before she could say more, Ròn with a heave on his flippers, lurched from the bogie on to the window shelf. Buckets and spades and balls went in all directions.

Mrs McColl was furious.

Katie Morag raced down the brae to catch the bouncing balls and bumped into the Holiday Children. They said they would help her take the seal pup back.

Katie Morag had a heavy heart as she pushed Ròn down to the water's edge. He flippered away into the sea. No mother came to meet him, within minutes he was back at Katie Morag's feet. She tried again to shove him off but the same thing happened again. Back he came! Her new friends cheered.

"We'll just have to look after you ourselves, then!" said Katie Morag, delighted with Ròn's return.

They sneaked him into the shed when no one was looking and got lots more seaweed for a bed. Mr McColl's barrel of salt herring was very convenient.

Feeding Ròn was difficult. He did not like the Ferryman's wife's chocolate cake but he scoffed left-over fish fingers from Katie Morag's tea, no bother at all. But Katie Morag didn't have fish fingers for tea every day. Soon the barrel of salt herring was empty.

"He eats an *awful* lot," said Jake.

"And he's not toilet trained," sniffed Jemma, "is he?"

"Well no..." agreed Katie Morag, wondering. Katie Morag was worried about the empty barrel but *most* worried about Ròn.

She and the Holiday Children tried dangling their fishing lines over the edge of the old pier but nobody caught anything.

"There are lots of fish in the sea," moaned Katie Morag, "but we are no good at catching them. I bet Ròn could though, if he really tried."

This time when Katie Morag pushed Ròn into the sea they all shouted and yelled when he came back. They banged bits of driftwood together and waved flags of torn netting. The seal looked a bit surprised but, eventually, he turned and headed out for the deep sea where the best fishes live.

Katie Morag was glad Ròn had gone home. She climbed slowly back up the brae to the shop and the Post Office.

"Can my friends come in for tea?" she asked.

"Of course!" said Mrs McColl.

"As long as they don't eat as much as Ròn..." smiled Mr McColl.

TOURIST INFORMATION

YOU
ARE
HERE

That night before she went to bed Katie Morag looked out of
her window. She was sure she saw Ròn's head in the bay –
or was it a beach-ball?